THIS BOOK BELONGS TO...

D1439520

TABLE OF CONTENTS

HOW TO DRAW

BEGINNER

INTERMEDIATE

ADVANCED

HOW TO DRAW

All you need is a pencil and an eraser.
For each drawing, you have a step by step diagram.

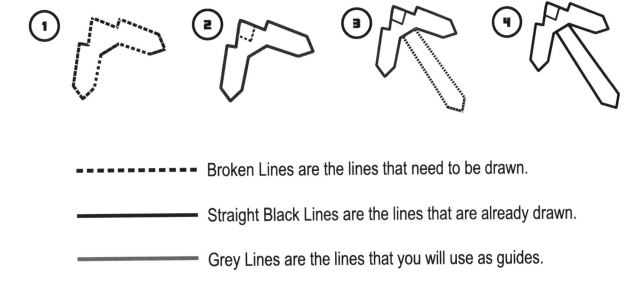

----------- Broken Lines are the lines that need to be drawn.

——————— Straight Black Lines are the lines that are already drawn.

═══════ Grey Lines are the lines that you will use as guides.

HOW TO USE THE BOOK

Use the blank pages on the right in order for you to practice.
Draw lightly at first, because you might need to erase some lines as you work.

Follow the diagrams for the details. Don't worry about being
perfect. An artist always make mistakes, they just find ways making them look
interesting.

KEEP PRACTICING AND YOU WILL GET BETTER

Once you finished your drawing in pencil, you can use a black fine
liner pen to trace it. You can color them too.

Enjoy learning to draw...

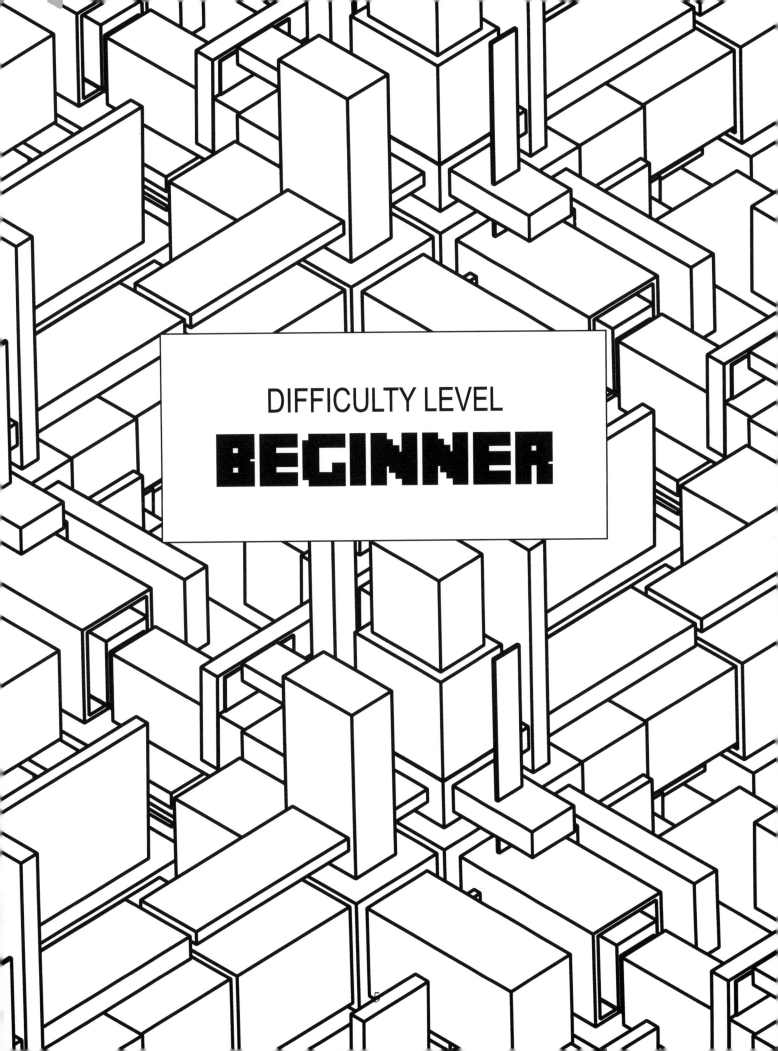

DIAMOND

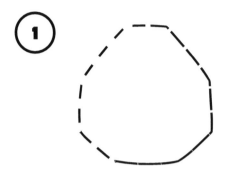

Begin by drawing the angled shape of your Minecraft diamond like so.

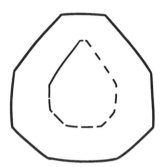

Next, you will draw in an angled tear drop shape on the inside of the diamond shape like so.

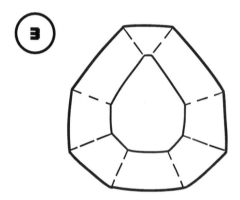

Lastly, create the texture of a diamond by drawing the simple lines around the tear drop.

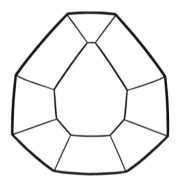

Here is your line art when finished. Now color in your Minecraft diamond.

USE THIS PAGE TO PRACTICE YOUR DRAWING

CAKE

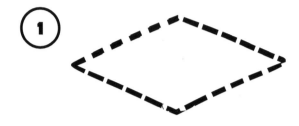

1   Take your ruler and make a box or square on a turned angle.

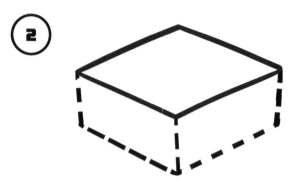

2   Draw in the bottom part of the cake, then add the detailing to make the object look three dimensional.

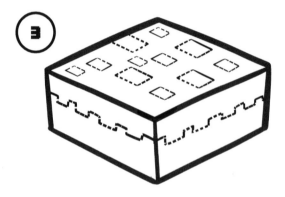

3   Lastly, draw the notched lining to form the frosting and then add the different shaped boxes on the top of the cake to finish it off.

4   Now you can color in your Minecraft cake.

USE THIS PAGE TO PRACTICE YOUR DRAWING

PICK

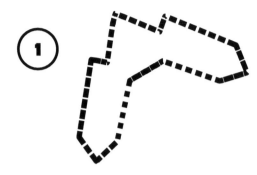

1

For the first step, all you have to do is draw the ax tip. This sort of looks like a three point mountain.

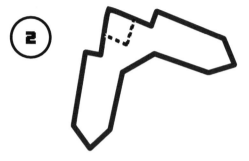

2

Add a detailing line which will separate the stone from the pole or handle.

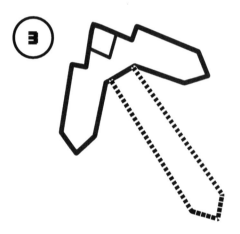

3

Lastly, draw in the rest of the pole or stick like so.

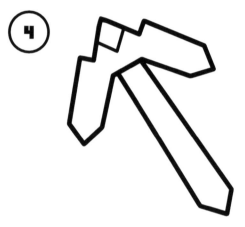

4

This is the line art when you are done. Now color in the Minecraft pick.

USE THIS PAGE TO PRACTICE YOUR DRAWING

STEVE FACE

1

Assuming that you are using a typical sized sheet of paper or canvas, the whole square will act as Steve's head. Having said that, start the first step by drawing the hairline for Steve. This is three straight lines at different levels.

2

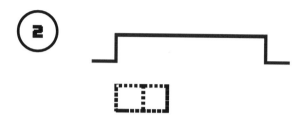

Here we will draw out the eye shape like so, then add a dividing line down the center.

3

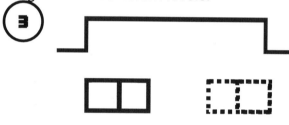

Next, draw in another eye the same way you did the first one.

4

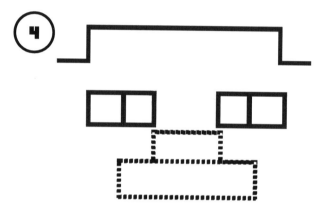

Up next and lastly, draw Steve's nose and mouth shapes.

5

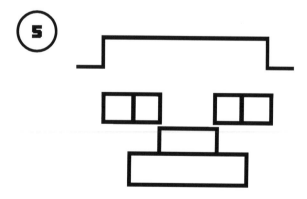

And that's all. There is it. Now you can color in Steve from Minecraft and bring him to life.

USE THIS PAGE TO PRACTICE YOUR DRAWING

LEARN HOW TO DRAW CUTE ANIMALS, FLOWERS AND MORE!

Just visit the link or scan the QR code we've provided below:

http://newbooks.space/howtodraw

- Open the camera app

- Focus the camera on the QR code by gently tapping the code

- Follow the instructions on the screen to complete the action

How To Draw:

All you need is a pencil and an eraser.
For each drawing, you have a step by step diagram.

DIAMOND SWORD

You will first draw the handle with the bottom knob being diamond shaped. Add the small handle.

Here you will draw the hand guard and notice how the ends are pointed and what else, diamond shaped.

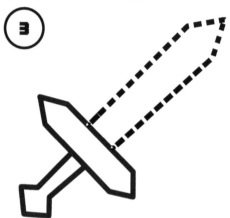

You will now draw the blade of the sword like so, then add the angled tip.

Sketch in the detailing to the sword down the middle of the blade, then add some dimensional lines to make the sword pop.

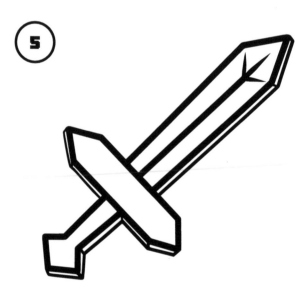

That's it, you are all done. Now you can color in your drawing and be on your way.

16

USE THIS PAGE TO PRACTICE YOUR DRAWING

CREEPER

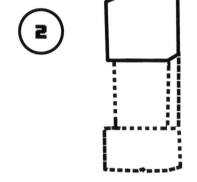

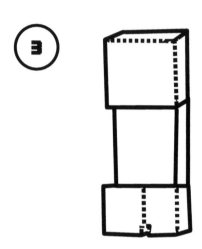

Start this first step by drawing a simple square shape.

Draw out the long blocky body like so, then make another square shape for the bottom of the Creeper's body

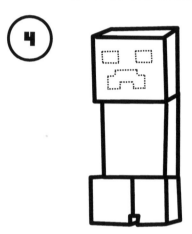

Detail the head like so, then draw the parting lines that will form the feet and or legs.

Lastly, draw in the digital face which is very simple as you can see.

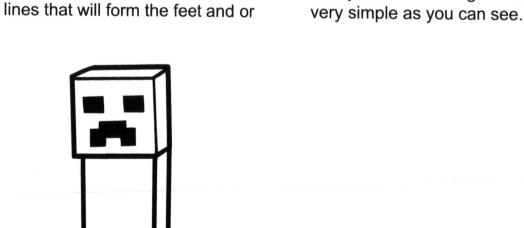

Here is your Creeper when you are all done drawing it out.

18

USE THIS PAGE TO PRACTICE YOUR DRAWING

ALEX

1 Start off with a square or box shape like so. This is for Alex's head.

2 Next, you will add the vertical line on the right to make her face or head dimensional. Once that is done draw in the boxy bangs, her eyes, mouth and rest of the hair.

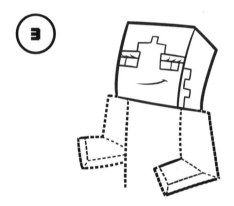

3 We will now draw the body. Start with the arms and torso. Add the dimensional lining for the arms.

4 Now you will add the lining for the clothing. Take your time because the lining is digital looking. Also add more detailing to the right arm.

5 For the final step, draw the rest of Alex's body which is the waist and legs. Add the clock lining to complete the design of her body.

6 Here is the line art when you are done. Now all you have to do is color Alex in and show someone who you just drew.

USE THIS PAGE TO PRACTICE YOUR DRAWING

PIG

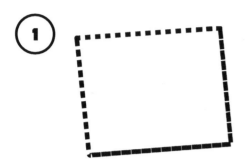

1 Make a square for the shape of the head.

2 Next, draw the boxy oblong shapes for the eyes, then draw the pig's nose and nostrils.

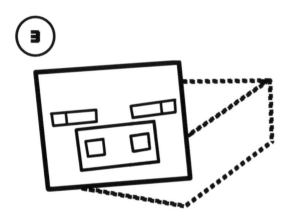

3 You will now draw the body which should be made in a flat box like style.

4 Draw the stubby boxy legs, then draw in the toe nails on the pig.

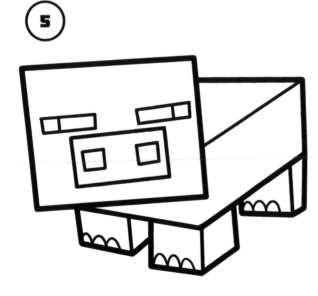

5 Here is the pig, now get your pig crayon, or marker to start coloring it in.

USE THIS PAGE TO PRACTICE YOUR DRAWING

USE THIS PAGE TO PRACTICE YOUR DRAWING

GHAST

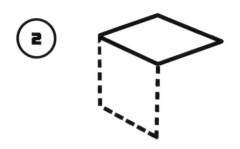

Make a box to start the lesson. This will be the starting point for the box shape of your Ghast.

Draw the front part of the Ghast's body like so.

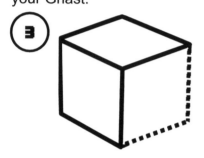

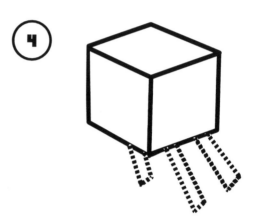

Close off the rest of the body by adding the last two lines. This will form the block body style.

Draw the first three tentacles like so. As you can see they look like flat noodles.

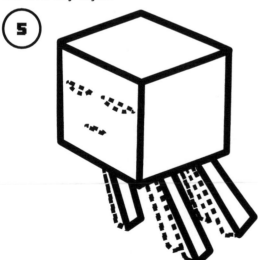

You will now draw the remainder of the limbs under the body like so, then draw in the digital style face which consists of closed looking eyes and a flat mouth line.

Here is the Ghast when you're done. Color it in white, and maybe have a fireball shooting out of its' mouth.

24

USE THIS PAGE TO PRACTICE YOUR DRAWING

OCELOT

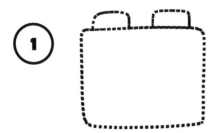

We will begin by drawing the square shaped head and then draw the tabs for the ears.

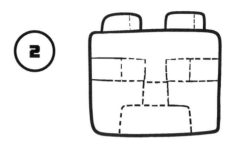

Next, draw the rectangular shapes for each eye and then draw the nose, ear and mouth lines.

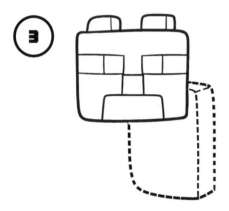

We will now create the chest of the Ocelot and then add that dimensional effect.

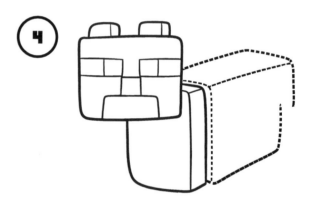

Go ahead and draw the length of the body.

Lastly, draw the blocky legs and then draw the Ocelot's tail.

That's it. You can now color in your Minecraft Ocelot.

USE THIS PAGE TO PRACTICE YOUR DRAWING

ZOMBIE

Begin by drawing a square block like so, then add the two dimensional detailing lines that will make the head look like a block.

Draw the eyes, and mouth like so, then add the tongue line.

You will now need to draw out the long arms and torso. Make sure that they are drawn in a blocky manner like you see here.

Next, add the detailing or definition lines on the arms and at the ends of each arm.

You will now finish this minecraft zombie by drawing out the hips, legs and then the bottoms of the feet. Add the detailing lines like so.

This is how your zombie looks when all is complete. Now you can color him in and be on your way.

USE THIS PAGE TO PRACTICE YOUR DRAWING

COW

1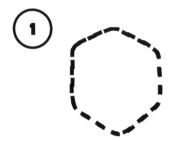

Here you will draw a octagon like shape, but it's actually a square.

2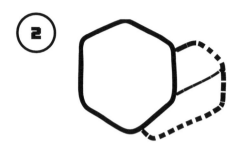

Next, draw the shape of the body which is shaped like a Twinkie, then add a definition line like so.

3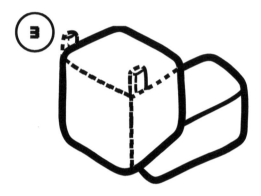

Box off the shape of the cow's head, then add the ears.

4

Now draw out the legs. Again, they look like mini Twinkies. Add detailing to the legs like so.

5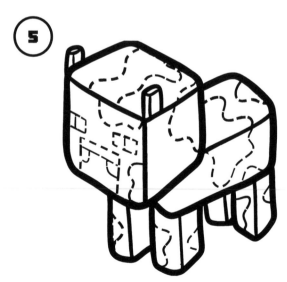

All you have to do here is draw in the cow pattern all over the cow's body and head. When that is done draw out the eyes, and nose.

6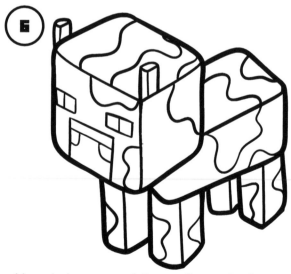

Here is how your Minecraft cow looks when you are done. Color it in, and show people that you can also draw characters from Minecraft as well as play the game.

USE THIS PAGE TO PRACTICE YOUR DRAWING

USE THIS PAGE TO PRACTICE YOUR DRAWING

VILLAGER

Start by making a rounded block shape for the head and be sure to add the dimensional look for this box or block.

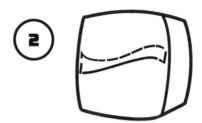

Next, our Minecraft villager has a unibrow so you will draw one wavy thick brow across the forehead like so.

Draw the nose in a long, block style.

Now draw the boxy shapes of the eyes. When the eyes are finished you can draw the frown for the mouth and add a frown line at the corners of the mouth.

Let's work on the body by drawing the arms and torso. The arms are crossed over one another as you can see here.

Add detailing to the shirt, then add dimension to the arm.

32

USE THIS PAGE TO PRACTICE YOUR DRAWING

7

Draw one whole shape for the legs in this step.

8

Now add the shirt line and dimensional line down the sides of the leg.

9

Make a split to give this villager two legs, then finish the shirt detailing.

10

Lastly, draw the blocky feet or shoes.

11

You are all done drawing your Minecraft villager. You can multiply this character.

USE THIS PAGE TO PRACTICE YOUR DRAWING

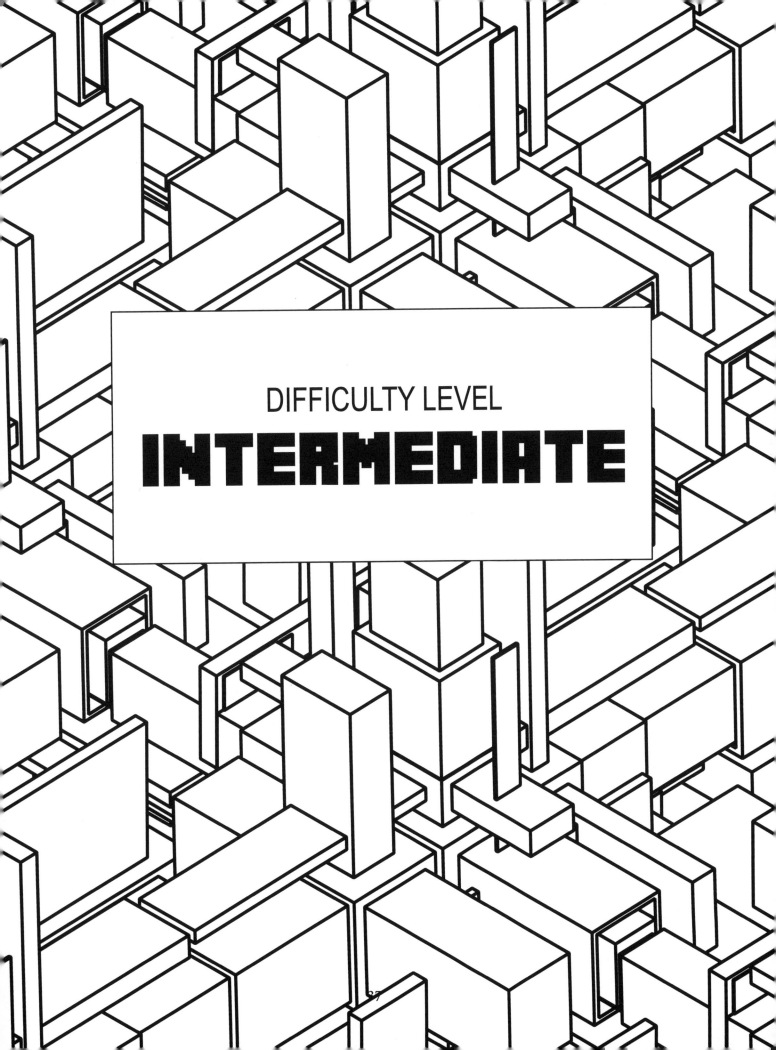

DIFFICULTY LEVEL

INTERMEDIATE

STEVE

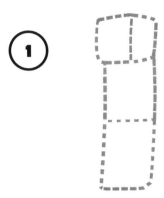

1. Make three blocks, as a guide, one for the head and two for the body.

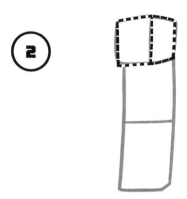

2. Define the block shape for Steve's head like so.

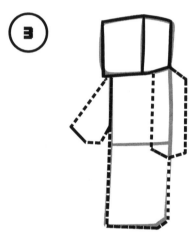

3. Next, grab your ruler if you need to and start drawing out the body first, then draw in the arms.

4. Next, draw in the digital looking hairline for Steve's hair, then draw in the face which is the eyes, nose and mustache.

5. Finish drawing Steve from Minecraft by making the lining to form the dimensional look for his limbs. Add the sleeve lines to the shirt, then draw the legs.

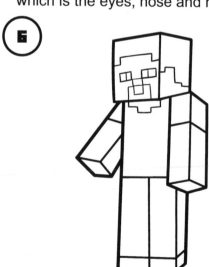

6. Erase the guideline, then you're done. For this character to really pop, you need to add some color to bring Steve to life.

USE THIS PAGE TO PRACTICE YOUR DRAWING

USE THIS PAGE TO PRACTICE YOUR DRAWING

HEROBRINE

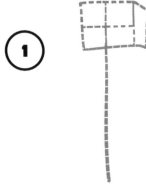

1 Start by drawing a box for the head, then sketch in the facial guidelines. You will then draw a vertical line for the body.

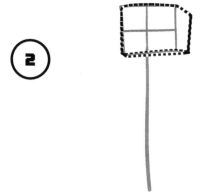

2 Define the shape of the head like so.

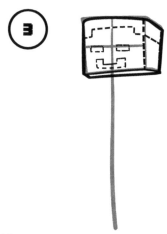

3 Here you will draw the lining to create the hair, then draw in the eyes and mouth.

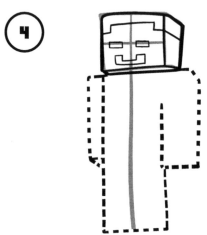

4 Draw the shoulders, thick arms, and stem like lower part of the body.

5 Add lines that will detail the body and form the clothing. This includes lining for the collar, sleeves, shirt line, then the pant cuff lines. When that is done you can add the block definition on the side of the body.

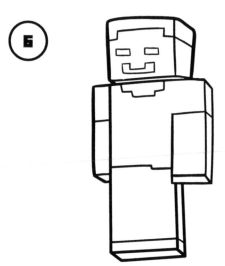

6 Erase the line, then that's it. Here is the line art for your Herobrine figure.

USE THIS PAGE TO PRACTICE YOUR DRAWING

ENDERMAN

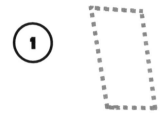

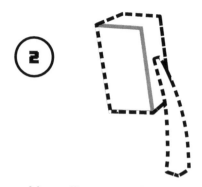

Start off with drawing a rectangular shaped guideline box like so. This will be for Enderman's face and body.

You will now us that same shape to draw out the block style body like so. When that is done draw in the long squared off arm.

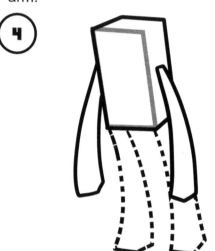

Draw in the other arm the very same way as well.

Next, draw the long, slender legs in a bent boxy manner as well.

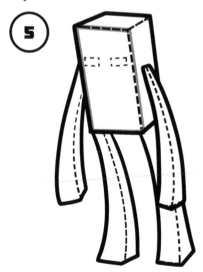

Lastly, draw in the digital eyes, and all the definition that will shape out his body.

Erase the guideline that you made. Here is what your Endermen looks like when finished. Now color it in to complete this drawing task,

USE THIS PAGE TO PRACTICE YOUR DRAWING

USE THIS PAGE TO PRACTICE YOUR DRAWING

WOLF

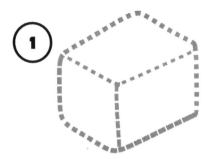

Like always we will start by making the guide shape for the wolf you are about to draw. This is in the form of a three dimensional block.

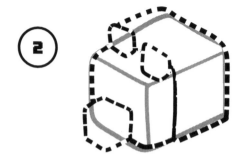

Using the shape you just made, begin drawing the structure of the head, then the face, and then the snout. The ears are last since they only rest on top of the wolf's head.

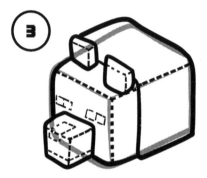

You will now draw in the face, as well as the mouth line and nose for the wolf's snout. Draw in the eyes, add the definition lining to the face, ears, and head to give the face and head that dim.

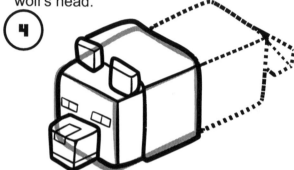

Almost done. All you need to do here is draw out the rectangular body followed by the tail.

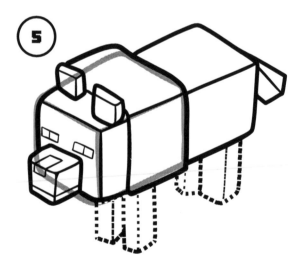

Lastly, draw the wolf's legs, then you are done after you erase the mistakes.

After you erase the guideline shape, now your Minecraft Wolf is ready to color in.

USE THIS PAGE TO PRACTICE YOUR DRAWING

CHICKEN

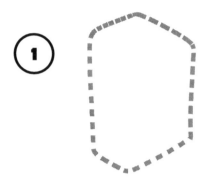

Make the oblong box guideline shape for the chicken's head.

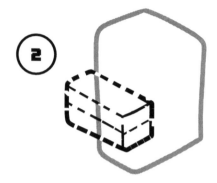

You will now draw the shape of the chicken's beak like so, followed by the lining that add depth.

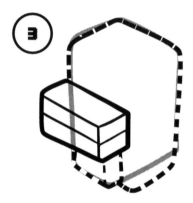

Outline the guideline shape you drew in step one but round it off at the edges. Draw the waddle which is the red sack hanging from under the beak.

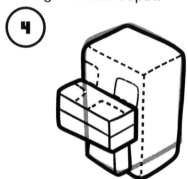

Add the eyes, draw the defining lines to shape out the head which will also look dimensional, then draw the holes on the beak as well.

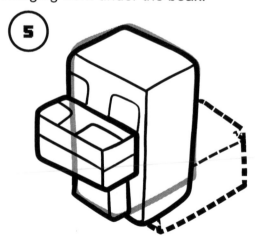

Almost done. You will need to draw out the body which is like a flat box. Add notches at the end of the chicken's body.

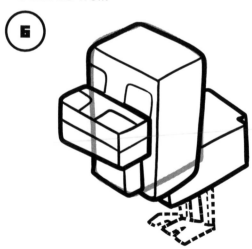

Lastly, draw the legs as well as the chicken's feet.

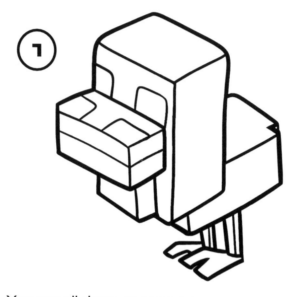

You are all done as soon as you erase
the guides. Here is your Minecraft
Chicken now. Now color it in

USE THIS PAGE TO PRACTICE YOUR DRAWING

SHEEP

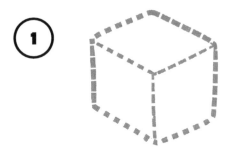

Draw a guideline box like so.

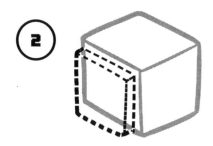

Next, make a flat panel like box on the front part of the sheep's head for the face.

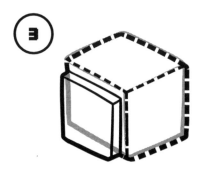

Simply darken the lining you made in step one for the head of the animal.

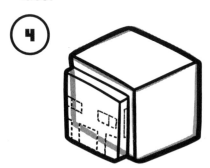

Draw in the eyes, nose, and the shapes for the cheeks. Don't forget to add extra shapes for the face.

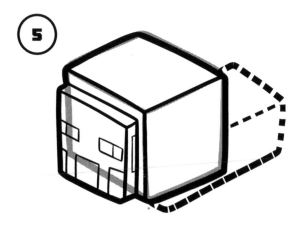

Draw out the rectangular box for the body.

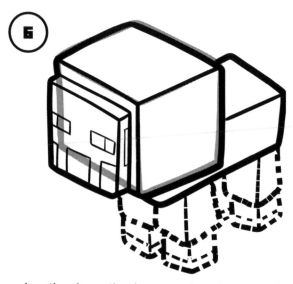

Lastly, draw the legs and make sure that you draw the overlapping parts of the leg which is also considered the thighs.

USE THIS PAGE TO PRACTICE YOUR DRAWING

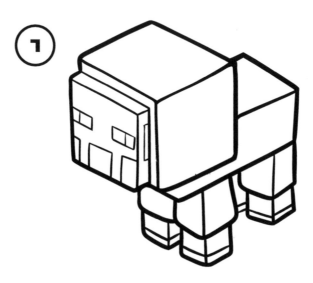

Erase the guideline box, then you can proceed. Here is the line art for the Minecraft Sheep you drew. Color in your sheep and that's it.

USE THIS PAGE TO PRACTICE YOUR DRAWING

USE THIS PAGE TO PRACTICE YOUR DRAWING

SKELETON

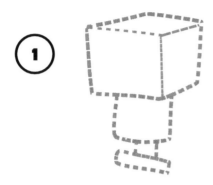

1 Draw a guideline box for the head of this skeleton, then draw the torso and lower body.

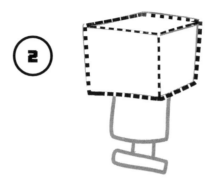

2 Define the shape of the head.

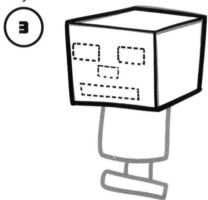

3 Next, draw in the eyes, nose and mouth which will remain hollow because they are just holes.

4 Here you will begin drawing the body starting with the torso. Notice how there is notches on the sides of the body or torso. Draw in the arms.

5 Add detailing to the arms to make them dimensional, then draw the detailing on the body. Lastly, draw the hip or pelvic bone then you will be done here.

6 Lastly, draw in the stick style legs, then you are all done.

USE THIS PAGE TO PRACTICE YOUR DRAWING

Erase the guideline, then that's it. Here is your Minecraft skeleton. You can begin coloring it in, or leave it like you see it.

USE THIS PAGE TO PRACTICE YOUR DRAWING

EXPLORE THE AMAZING DINO AGE!

Just visit the link or scan the QR code we've provided below to color your favorite dinosaur.

http://newbooks.space/dino

- Open the camera app

- Focus the camera on the QR code by gently tapping the code

- Follow the instructions on the screen to complete the action

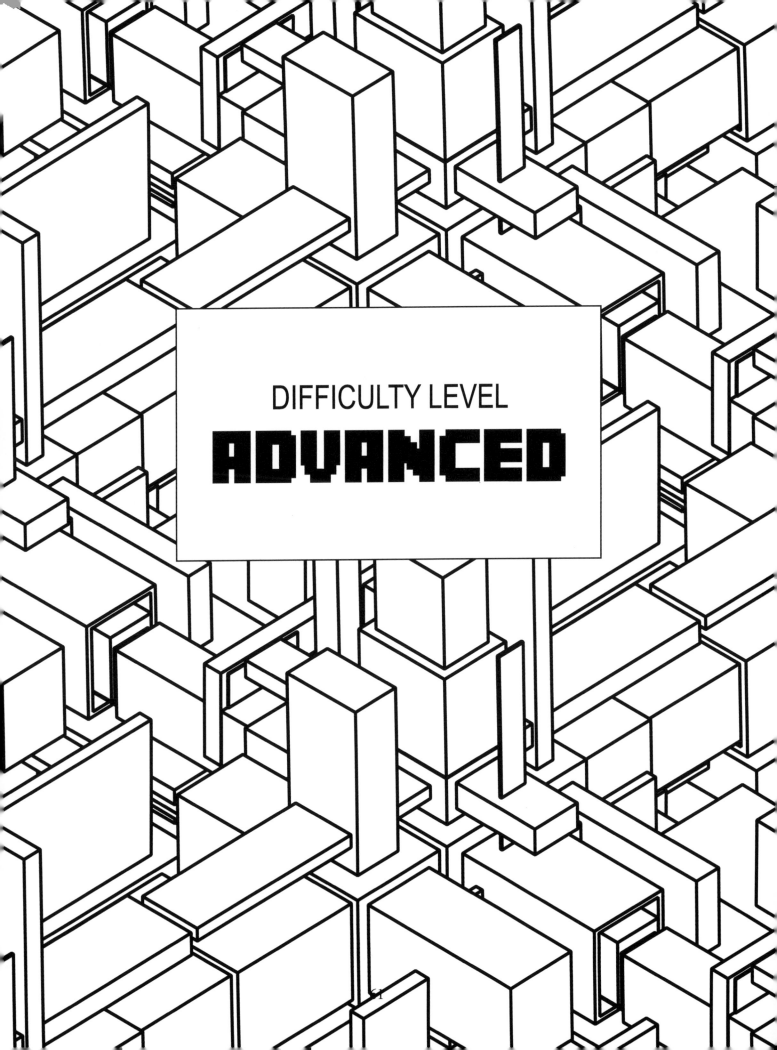

CAVE SPIDER

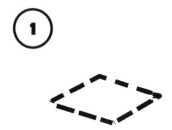

1

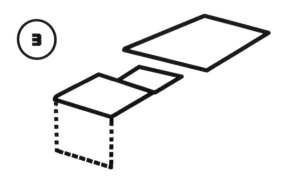

First step is to make a flat looking square like so. This will be the beginning of the spider's head.

2

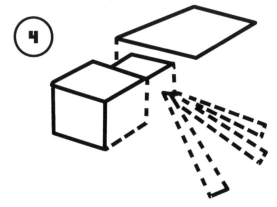

Here you will draw two more boxes. As you can see the back one is bigger than the one in the center. These squares will form the body.

3

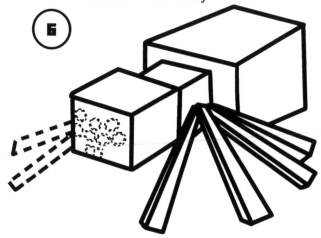

Begin squaring off the head by drawing yet another box. You will keep doing this until blocks are formed.

4

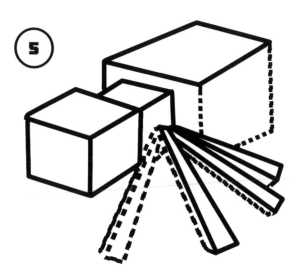

Close off the head, and the mid section like so. When that is done you can draw the twig like legs that should remain clumped together at the base where the limbs attach to the body.

5

Draw in one more leg so you will have a total of four. When that is complete you will define the legs so they look two dimensional. Draw or finish the back part of the spiders body.

6

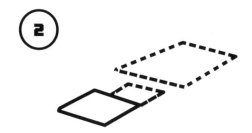

Draw the other legs on the opposite side of the spider's body, then draw a total of seven round eyes followed by the fangs.

USE THIS PAGE TO PRACTICE YOUR DRAWING

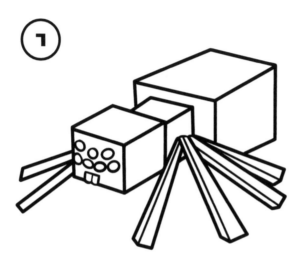

Here is what the spider looks like when you are all done. Now you can color it in and add this drawing to your Minecraft sketch book.

USE THIS PAGE TO PRACTICE YOUR DRAWING

SKY ARMY

First, begin by sketching the basic guidelines for Sky. Make sure you try to draw these guidelines accurately in order to achieve a successful outcome. Take your time and try to refrain from rushing. Draw these guidelines lightly.

Then, sketch the block head for Sky, keeping in mind that he has hair framing the outer corner of his head.

Next, using swift and light strokes, sketch the pieces of hair which frame his face. Don't forget that line which adds a dimensional border to the head.

Next, sketch the facial features for Sky, making sure the glasses are dimensionally correct as the perspective of the face.

Let's move onto sketching the body shape for Sky by first beginning with the right arm and then moving onto the middle body shape. After you've drawn those two in that order, sketch the left arm. Drawing from this execution will aid you at drawing an accurate form of Sky.

66

Now, this is going to be a big step to draw, mainly because of all the inner detailing. Take your time with this part, because the detailing is what makes Sky's character. Draw the inner detailing with thinner line weights to achieve a variety within the lineart piece.

USE THIS PAGE TO PRACTICE YOUR DRAWING

USE THIS PAGE TO PRACTICE YOUR DRAWING

(7)

Lastly, sketch the block-like legs and then the details which create a blocky appearance for Sky. Take your time! I know the last step will get you on the edge.

(8)

Before you get a pen or marker to ink your drawing, proof check your drawing to make sure that everything is anatomically correct. Remember to use various line weights for certain lines to add variety. Thick lines for the outside, and thin lines for the inner detailing lines.

USE THIS PAGE TO PRACTICE YOUR DRAWING

WITHER SKELETON

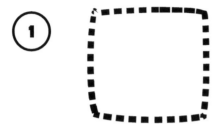

1 Draw a square for the head.

2 Next, draw and color in the slanted eyes and nose, then draw the skeletal style mouth which is teeth. Add the dents on the face as well around the mouth and cheeks.

3 Next, draw the chest or torso which is in the form of a rib cage.

4 Sketch in the detailing to the rib cage, then add some bone definition on the rib bones.

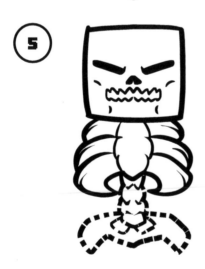

5 Continue to sketch in the body in the form of bones. Draw the hip or pelvic bones.

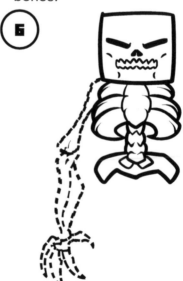

6 Next, draw the long bony arm from the top, all the way down to the skeletal fingers.

70

USE THIS PAGE TO PRACTICE YOUR DRAWING

USE THIS PAGE TO PRACTICE YOUR DRAWING

7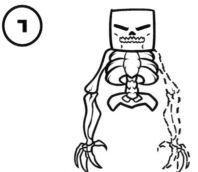

Draw in the other arm the same way you drew the first one to the tee.

8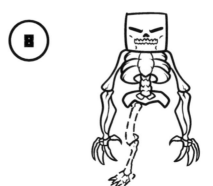

We will get started with drawing the thigh bone, then the lower leg bone. Draw in the feet which is in the form of, you guessed it, bones.

9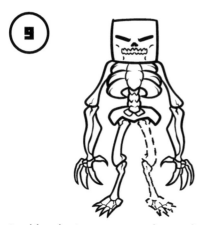

And lastly, just repeat the task at hand the same way you draw the first leg and foot. Add the detailing where needed.

10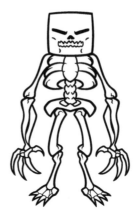

Here is the wither skeleton from Minecraft. Now you can have fun coloring this figure in black.

USE THIS PAGE TO PRACTICE YOUR DRAWING

USE THIS PAGE TO PRACTICE YOUR DRAWING

ZOMBIE PIGMAN

Draw a square for the head which also looks like a block.

Next, draw two circles for the eyes, then draw in a pig nose. You will need to color in the nostrils. Add the bags under the eyes.

Here you will draw the cracked looking lines on the face which will also define the zombie style face. Draw in the skeletal teeth for the mouth.

You will now draw the torso, and when you do this make sure the rib on the left side is exposed. Draw the crooked lining to form the ripped or rotted flesh.

You will now draw out the arms, then add dimension to them by adding the lining and square tips.

Finish drawing the body by forming the legs and squared off feet.

USE THIS PAGE TO PRACTICE YOUR DRAWING

USE THIS PAGE TO PRACTICE YOUR DRAWING

Here you will draw the lining on both sides of legs which will make the legs look boxy or square. Add more torn flesh.

Add the last of the detailing and then you are done. The bone in the center of the leg is exposed.

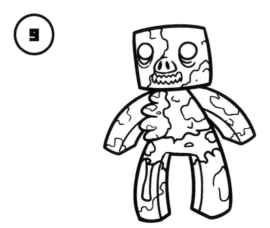

Here is the line art when you are finished. Now you can color zombie Pigman in.

FULLY LOADED COMPLETE ACTIVITY BOOK

Just visit the link or scan the QR code we've provided below to check out the Fortniter How to Draw, Coloring Pages, Puzzles and other activity book!

http://newbooks.space/fortniter

- Open the camera app

- Focus the camera on the QR code by gently tapping the code

- Follow the instructions on the screen to complete the action

ENDER DRAGON

The first thing we will do is draw a box shape for the head of this dragon.

Next, turn the square shape into a box like so.

Draw in Ender Dragon's snout in a boxy manner.

We will now draw in the eyes, nostrils, and then the ears. As you can see the ears are rounded.

You will now draw Ender Dragon's neck which should be long and not too skinny. Once that is done you can add some spikes on the back of the neck.

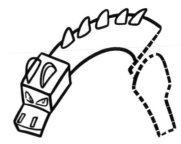

Next, draw a straight line to form the base of the neck, then draw out the shoulder and some of the front leg.

USE THIS PAGE TO PRACTICE YOUR DRAWING

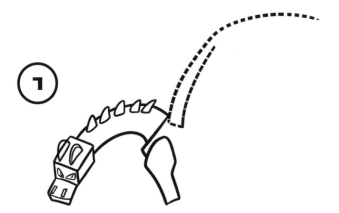

7

Get started with drawing the arched wing.

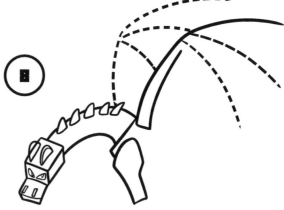

8

Once you have one of the large arched wings drawn, you can add the spine like pieces that will hold the wing in place. These are fingers for a dragon's wing.

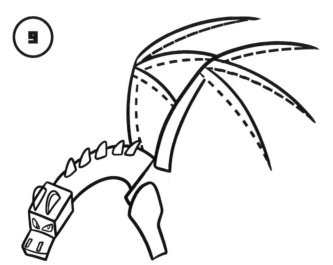

9

Define the fingers or bones on the wings like so to give them shape and structure.

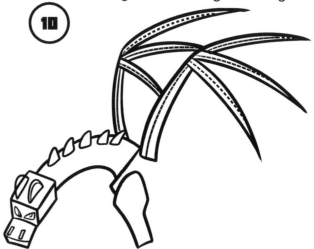

10

Add more detailing to the wing bones.

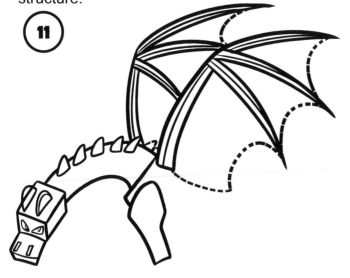

11

Now you can fill in the wing with a web like pattern. The base of the wing will form some of the back for the Ender Dragon.

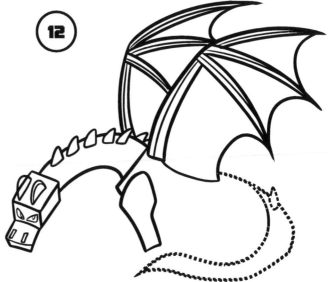

12

Now we can tackle the task of drawing more of the back line followed by the tail. Add one spike on the tail.

USE THIS PAGE TO PRACTICE YOUR DRAWING

USE THIS PAGE TO PRACTICE YOUR DRAWING

Here you will only have to add more spikes down the shape of Ender Dragon's tail.

Define the tail like so to make it dimensional.

Let's get started by drawing more of the body. When the stomach is drawn, draw in the front paws or feet like so.

Draw the back legs in a rounded manner. You will also need to draw the feet too.

Almost done folks. Add detailing to the body to make the Ender Dragon look blocky. Define the legs, back and feet.

Add some large sharp claws on each foot like so, and be sure to take your time so they come out looking thick and sort of realistic.

84

USE THIS PAGE TO PRACTICE YOUR DRAWING

Finally for the last drawing step all you have to do is draw in the definition to the front shoulder above the leg.

Here is how your drawing should come out looking when you are done. Now you can color in Ender Dragon black with green eyes.

USE THIS PAGE TO PRACTICE YOUR DRAWING

USE THIS PAGE TO PRACTICE YOUR DRAWING

CLAIM YOUR BONUS:

WWW.BONUS-GIVE.COM/MINECRAFT

Printed in Great Britain
by Amazon